THERE AND BACK

THERE AND BACK

A COLLECTION OF SECRET DOOR SHORT STORIES

ELI BAILEY   HAILEY BROWN   JR. BUNCH

ETHAN HERROD   ANNA CLAIRE JACKSON

ALYSSA KINKADE   NOAH LEE

SARAH MURLEY   MCCAIN ROBERTS

JACK STEVENSON   BAILEY STROUD

HALLE VINCENT   EDEN WAGNON

LAYLA WALL

Edited by
AL AINSWORTH

Family Story Legacy Publishing

Visit www.familystorylegacypublishing.com.

DEDICATIONS

To our Creator God for forming us in Your image
with the gifts of wonder and imagination
and for including us in the greatest story every told.

Eli Bailey
To Mr. Ainsworth, for guiding me in my writing of
"My Struggles in Austin."

Hailey Brown
To my parents, for teaching me to always try my
hardest and encouraging me to write this story.

Jr. Bunch
To Mr. Ainsworth, for inspiring my ideas.

Ethan Herrod
To my parents, for encouraging me in this project.
To Mr. Ainsworth, for assisting me on it.

Anna Claire Jackson
To Caroline Court, for being the best Jo.

Alyssa Kinkade
To my mom and dad, for encouraging me through the process of writing this story.
To Ollie and Layla, for helping me edit my story.

Sarah Murley
To Mom and Dad, for teaching me to be determined, hardworking, and diligent throughout my life.

McCain Roberts
To Mom and Dad, for pushing me to work hard.
To my family and friends, who helped me through this process.
To Mr. Ainsworth, for giving me this opportunity .

Bailey Stroud
To my dad and mom, for teaching me to always conquer my fears and for encouraging me while I wrote this story.

Halle Vincent
To Mom and Dad, for encouraging me to reach my fullest potential.
To MawMaw and PawPaw, for cheering me on.
To Mrs. Heun, for inspiring and fostering my love for writing.

Eden Wagnon
To Mom and Sarah Murley, who both encouraged me every step of the way.
To Mr. Ainsworth, who made this possible.
To God, who inspired me through His Word.

Layla Wall
To my mom and sister, for telling me this story was great (even before it was).

Al Ainsworth
To Jonathan Bunch, for casting the vision that I would one day help others tell their stories. How poetic that your son is one of our debut authors.

ACKNOWLEDGMENTS

*Thank you to the DeSoto Excellence in
Education foundation for assisting
teachers go beyond their curricula and
classroom budgets to do special projects
like this one.*

*Thank you to Barry Bouchillon and State
Farm for funding our grant and for your
excitement about seeing it to fruition.*

*Thank you to Carol Burton for partnering
with us to make this grant a reality.*

*Thank you to the authors of this collection
for going above and beyond your
academic and extracurricular demands to
make this collection a reality.*

CONTENTS

Introduction   xiii

1. My Struggles in Austin   1
   Eli Bailey
2. Vera and Lily   5
   Hailey Brown
3. Comfort Zone   13
   Jr. Bunch
4. Jorge and the Secret Door   17
   Ethan Herrod
5. Some Things Are Meant To Be   25
   Anna Claire Jackson
6. The Perfect World   33
   Alyssa Kinkade
7. The Electric Guitar Odyssey   39
   Noah Lee
8. Saving Josef   45
   Sarah Murley
9. Mary and Me   53
   McCain Roberts
10. The Locker to Alterworld   59
    Jack Stevenson
11. Unbearably Afraid   67
    Bailey Stroud
12. The Family Portrait   73
    Halle Vincent
13. She and Her People   79
    Eden Wagnon
14. To the Moon And To Saturn   91
    Layla Wall

About the Authors   97

INTRODUCTION

A lengthy break to pursue other interests interrupted my twenty-plus years in the English classroom. During that time, I wrote my first book and continued to write until my books now number more than a dozen. One book into my writing career, a new friend looked me in the eye and said, "You're going to help people tell their stories."

Over the last few years, I have assisted several people in writing and publishing their first books. It is now my pleasure to present this collection of short stories from my tenth-grade students at Northpoint Christian School. Allow me to share a little background on this project. My favorite lesson each year is based on author Mac Barnett's TED Talk "Why a Good Book Is a Secret Door." In that video, Barnett calls the willing suspension of disbelief the key to enjoying fiction. I use Barnett's talk to introduce a narrative writing unit but also to extend Barnett's ideas to the wider scope of education and faith.

I hung the letters D-I-S-B-E-L-I-E-F from the ceiling in my classroom at the start of this school year, a literal suspension of disbelief, before teaching the concept throughout the school year. To their credit, my students bought into this idea through their willingness to learn and try new things.

Our secret door narrative unit coincided with the DeSoto Excellence in Education's annual teacher grant application process. To help my students share their stories, I applied for the funds to produce this anthology. Several months later, we won the grant! My students and I have now published these stories in both e-book and print formats. The fifth-grade students at our school will receive paperback copies of this book and engage in lessons from it.

Each story follows the same basic structure, based on Donald Miller's basic story outline. A character has a problem (external and internal/psychological). After going through a secret door of some sort into another world, the character meets a guide, who gives the protagonist a plan and calls him or her to action. The main character then returns to the original world through a secret door, ready to work the plan. The ending can be positive (a comedy) or negative (a tragedy). Although the external problems vary widely, the internal/psychological problems of the protagonists in these stores touch on basic human issues like loneliness, fear, and the desire to overcome.

The students represented in this collection have gone beyond the writing process to learn about publishing. They have edited their works, worked through an editing program to improve their stories, and subjected their works to my editing. They have learned about formatting, e-book and paperback covers, and submitting a manuscript. The fourteen students who completed the writing and publishing processes to produce this book are all first-time authors. Once upon a time, a friend told me I would help people tell their stories. I am proud to present the stories of these debut authors and hopeful that these stories won't be their last.

Al Ainsworth, Editor

MY STRUGGLES IN AUSTIN
ELI BAILEY

I really miss Memphis. Austin is great, but I miss walking through downtown Memphis during the night with all my buddies. Those were the good days. It has been a year since I moved to Austin, and I haven't been able to make any real friends from school. I'll just go ask Cameron for help. Oh, wait, he's in Nashville with Mom. Man, I miss him. He was a brother who knew exactly what to say and gave brilliant advice.

My parents were never good at that. It didn't get better when they divorced two years ago. It still feels as if it happened yesterday. I mean, I still forget Cameron doesn't live in the same place as me anymore. I always admired my brother because my dad never had time to help me. He would say things like, "Luke, not now, I'm working!" or "Luke, you're fifteen, you can handle it yourself!" He was always working and I wish he had more time for me. The next school year starts tomorrow, and I would do anything to ask Cameron for advice about making friends.

I started my day off a little late, 11:30 a.m. to be exact. I ate some cereal and walked back into my room to read a book by my favorite sports author. In the middle of reading a chapter about throwing a baseball, I closed my eyes and remembered the memories my brother and I had made when he taught me how to throw a baseball. I have a good imagination, but after a few throws, I realized I was not imagining any more. This was real!

With a tear in my eye, I ran up to him and gave him a hug. He hugged me while questioning what was happening. I realized we were re-living the moment in our backyard where we were throwing a baseball after watching the Yankees' game. We began throwing the baseball, and I told him about how lonely I was at school.

"How did you make friends when you and Mom

moved away?" He and Mom had moved away a year earlier than Dad and I, which meant he had gone through the same problem as me.

"It is not a simple task. It took a month or two before I had my first real friend. Pick people who are like you. Once you make those few friends, you make plans with them, plans which involve after-school activities. Then you will meet their friends, your group will expand, and you will get invited to different hangouts. I was lucky to have met another new kid named Anthony. We became good friends because we were both lonely and in a new city."

I wish I could meet someone like Anthony. Cameron told me a couple of great conversation starters to get me started. Then he threw the ball over my head and into the trees behind me. When I returned, he was gone.

I rubbed my eyes to make sure I was seeing right, and when I stopped and opened them, I was back in Austin reading my book. After I finished the book, I decided I would try out what Cameron had told me.

I woke up the next morning and did all my morning routines before leaving for school. Eager to make friends, I walked into chemistry class and sat down next to a kid who looked as lonely I felt and used some of the conversation starters Cameron had told me about. I couldn't believe it, but it worked; I made my first friend! His name is Ethan, and he is hilarious and an overall fun guy to be with. I tried this in every one of my other classes, and sometimes it worked and sometimes it didn't. I still had a hard time believing I made three friends on my first day! Maybe this school year won't turn out to be so bad after all. No more lonely Austin, Texas, for me.

VERA AND LILY

HAILEY BROWN

$\mathcal{A}$fter her parents died, Vera Kelley moved in with her Aunt Chrissy. Aunt Chrissy was cruel to her niece, forcing her to wash, iron, cook, and clean. Vera cried herself to sleep every night in her room, alone. She didn't want to cause a fuss, so she suffered in silence in the face of her aunt's bullying. This only spurred her aunt to become more inhumane, until one day, her aunt crossed the line. "You are just like your mother—rude, callous, and pathetic! No one will ever love or respect you."

Vera had never been so heartbroken. Whenever Aunt Chrissy got this way, Vera ran to her secret spot, a hidden cove along the west side of her aunt's estate, where she could get away from her aunt's mockery. Vera's mother went there as a child, and it gave Vera a sense of protection and comfort when she came here. Vera often laid a towel on the sand and read for hours on end. She enjoyed reading because it allowed her to escape reality by envisioning herself in the worlds created by books.

Vera particularly loved reading the story of Cinderella. Oh, how she wished to be in her place. Vera knew Cinderella had problems too, but at least Cinderella got her happily ever after. This gave Vera hope that she, too, would be like Cinderella—that someday her struggles would disappear, and she would have a happy ending of her own.

Vera saw a glimmer of light down by the rocks while she was reading and went to see what it was. She discovered a beautiful locket that had washed up on the shore. She had seen nothing quite like it, so she looped the chain around her neck. As she did this, her legs grew weak, and she felt faint. Vera suddenly passed out and hit the ground.

Vera woke up, falling from the sky and heading straight to the ground. She had never been here before. The sky was a light purple, and everything was peaceful, almost too peaceful. In the distance,

Vera saw a young lady with wavy blonde hair looking into the sky. She was using her binoculars to see what fell out of the sky. The lady walked up to Vera. She had a gentle appearance and a soft smile.

"Excuse me, my name is Lily. Are you alright? You had quite a fall."

"I'm okay. My name is Vera Kelley. I was reading outside of my house, and the next thing I know, I'm here. Where am I exactly?"

"I have a lot to explain. Come with me to my house, and I will answer all of your questions."

Vera followed Lily to a lovely house, secluded from the rest of the area. Lily explained to Vera that they were on Planet Cyrus. That was the ruler's name. King Cyrus trapped anyone who found their way to the planet and sealed them off from the rest of the world.

"So Vera, you were reading outside of your house, fell asleep, and woke up here?" asked Lily, ever so kindly.

"Yes, and I also found this locket. It looks strange, but I like it. One side has a pretty gem on it. Too bad it won't open."

"Do you mind if I look at that?"

Vera didn't want to take it off since she had never

owned something like that before; however, she allowed Lily to peer at it around her neck.

"Why, Vera! This might sound crazy, but that's the locket of Queen Ophelia!" said Lily.

"Who's she?"

"Queen Ophelia is the king's wife. It's said that her missing locket is what can get us off this planet! I have been searching for that locket for years, and now we only have to find the hidden key to unlock it. But Vera, stay here at my house. If that locket gets in the wrong hands, it could lead to trouble."

Vera sat down at the table and told Lily all about her life at home. She had never opened up to anyone before, but Lily was such a loving and understanding person. Lily gave Vera the advice that just because you're little, you don't have to let people walk over you.

"You mustn't let being small stop you from doing great things. When we get back to earth, I will find you and take you away from your wicked aunt," said Lily.

Vera felt loved for the first time in her life. She had to get that key not only for herself but for Lily, of whom she grew so fond. Vera woke up every morning for several weeks in search of the missing key. But one day, Vera went inside earlier than usual. She found a journal left open in the study.

It read, *I'm so close to getting off this place, but poor Vera thinks she'll leave, too! There is no way she is going home this quickly, especially since they locked me on this planet, alone, for hundreds of years. She's been searching for this "missing key," but actually, I've had it with me the whole time. I found it years ago. I just need to lure her in and get the locket at the right moment. Then I'll place the key in the locket and leave her here!*

Little did Vera know, Lily wrote the page weeks before, but had reconsidered. Lily learned a lot from Vera. Vera never had a caring, nurturing family that most children grow up with, and she always had to depend on herself for everything. This type of situation would turn many people bitter, but not Vera. Instead, she did everything she could do to spread peace and happiness with others. Lily gained a new outlook on life thanks to her, but Vera did not know this yet. At that moment, Vera still thought the page was correct. She rushed out of the room, her eyebrows furrowed. She found Lily sitting in the living room.

"You lied to me, Lily! And I trusted no one more than you! Please give me the key so I can go home!" shouted Vera.

Lily's heart sank. She needed to make things right with Vera.

"I regret everything I have done wrong, and I'm sorry. You changed me, Vera. You taught me that even when you're in unpleasant situations, you make the best out of it. Let's leave now. I have the key right here." She pulled the key out of her drawer. "This will transport us back to where we came from, but I promise I will find you." Vera saw that look of sincerity on Lily's face and accepted her apology. They both touched the locket. Lily put the key in it, and the world turned black for a second.

The two then woke up in their homes on earth. Two months passed before Vera saw Lily again, but she lived with the hope Lily would find her one day. As Vera was reading in her room one afternoon, she heard a knock on the door. It was Lily! Having worked out the details with Aunt Chrissy, Lily arranged for Vera to be cared for by her. Vera, who had never experienced such joy in her life, ran to hug Lily as her tears rolled down her cheeks.

Vera then led an extraordinary childhood with her new guardian. She became the top of her class, read all the books she wanted, and never saw her evil Aunt Chrissy again. As for the locket, Vera kept it in a safe place. Even though that locket caused danger, it still was the one thing that changed Vera's life forever.

3
———

COMFORT ZONE
JR. BUNCH

*H*ey, I'm Milo. I'm a thirteen-year-old boy who enjoys anime, but the kids at my school don't. Nobody talks to me because they assume I'm weird. I also don't have any friends because I struggle with social anxiety. Today is the first day back from Christmas break, and I awakened extremely nervous. Before I left for school, I watched my favorite show, *Chun-Ti*. Watching this show always brings me joy. I regularly ponder about how much better life would be if I lived in *Chun-Ti*. When the show was over, I said goodbye to my parents. They did not respond, so I left. My parents are so consumed by work that they sometimes forget that I even exist.

I walked to school, nervous about seeing

everyone again. When I arrived, I made my way to class. In first period, everyone was talking about what they got for Christmas, while I sat there with no one to talk to. Later, at lunch, one kid did not seem familiar, so I supposed he was new to our school. I thought, this is my opportunity to make a friend. I wanted to talk to him, but I was too nervous. Instead, I just continued to eat my lunch.

Later that night at my basketball game, I couldn't find my parents in the stands. That crushed my spirits, but I tried to stay focused on the game. As the ball tipped off, our starting point guard, Peter Jones, advanced the ball up to me for a wide-open layup. As the ball dropped through the net, I came down awkwardly and tweaked my ankle. I lay on the floor as my coach came and helped me off the court. The game went back and forth throughout, but we lost. It was tough watching my team and not being able to play. After the game, I called my parents to pick me up. I thought, they don't even care. Soon my dad pulled up, and I hopped in.

"Where were y'all?" I asked.

"We forgot," he said.

I put my head down as tears rolled down my face. When we got home, I ran up the stairs to my room. The only thing that would comfort me was *Chun-Ti*.

When I pulled up the show on my laptop, it seemed like the main character, Ni, was talking directly to me. He said, "Press the enter key to set foot into the world of *Chun-Ti*."

When I pressed enter, I zapped through my laptop screen and I was in *Chun-Ti*. Glancing around, I saw Ni standing a few feet away from me. I needed to go back home, but before I left, I wanted to ask Ni if he could help me with my social skills. Ni smiled at me as I walked over.

I said, "Hey, it is so cool to meet you; this is unbelievable!"

"You seem worried. Are you okay?"

"To be honest, I'm struggling with my social skills."

He replied, "Great, I can help you. Let's get started. First, when talking or approaching someone, stay calm and take a deep breath. Second, look them in the eye when talking to them. To sum it up, when talking to people, be kind and hold an extensive conversation with them."

I responded, "You are the best. I appreciate your advice."

"No problem."

He snapped his fingers, and I was back in my room.

"That was great," I said. Then I turned to go to sleep. The next morning, I smelled breakfast when I woke up. I came downstairs and my parents were cooking breakfast.

"Good morning, son," they said from the table.

"Hey, Mom and Dad."

"There's enough for you," my dad said.

I ate and left for school. They're different, I thought.

Later at lunch, there was that new kid from yesterday sitting in the same spot. This time I would take advantage of my opportunity and talk to him. I walked over to him and we exchanged greetings.

Then I asked, "Do you enjoy anime?"

"Yes," he responded.

My eyes lit up with excitement. "Me, too." We walked out of the lunchroom together, discussing our favorite anime characters.

4

JORGE AND THE SECRET DOOR

ETHAN HERROD

*J*orge Rodriguez's black eyes looked on in sorrow and confusion as Enrique stormed in and threw himself on the couch. He asked no questions about what troubled his older brother, but the problem had already become apparent to him. Enrique had once again failed to find employment and would soon face eviction. Jorge remembered the last time they were homeless. Strangers stared at them, avoided them, and showed no signs of goodwill. The feeling of being less than made Jorge recoil in fear.

"Enrique," began Jorge, "if you don't get hired soon, will we be back out there again?" He couldn't bring himself to say *homeless*.

"No, Jorge. We will stay right here. Even if I don't find a job, we can always sell the watch."

Jorge knew Enrique did not believe his own words. Enrique's mention of selling their father's watch had shocked him; though it was golden and valuable, it was the only possession they still had from their parents. As he got ready for bed later that night, Jorge knew he must fix their predicament.

Enrique woke early the next morning. After making his brother breakfast, he ventured out once more to locate any work he could find. Jorge, however, was not to have such a repetitive schedule. He equipped himself with a jacket and tattered shoes and, instead of staying home within a safe distance of his neighbors, as usual, left the apartment to find work of his own.

Jorge trekked across the concrete jungle until coming to an area more populated than his own. He bounded from one business to another, attempting to earn money to assist his brother. As the day passed with no success, Jorge resorted to soliciting individuals. This, too, ended in failure. He noticed a change in the surrounding atmosphere as the day progressed. The passersby appeared repulsed by Jorge's mere presence, glaring at his ragged apparel and examining the scars on his arms. Their contempt reminded him of the treatment he received when he and Enrique had first become impoverished. The pressure of their stares became too much for him, and he fled the inner city.

After running and running without a discernible direction, Jorge arrived in an abandoned part of the city that was riddled with unfinished homes and apartments. Still wishing to maintain his livelihood, he wandered throughout the desolate abodes, hoping to see something of value he could take with him. A small apartment caught his attention, spurring him to go in. The inside was wet and dark, covered with holes and stains that encouraged Jorge to reconsider his action; however, through one door emerged an ethereal, captivating light. Jorge resisted his better instincts and approached the door while twisting the knob. The light continued to shine, obscuring any sight of what was inside. Curious, he stepped through the door and found himself inside a closet.

Jorge forced his way out and gazed at his new surroundings, which resembled a neglected basement. While making his way across the wooden floor and up the ivory stairs, the boy faced impressive scenery.

Jorge entered a room of fancy suits and impressive accessories from a long-forgotten time. He was still taking in the amazing room when a cold, clammy hand grabbed him. Spinning around, Jorge encountered an unwelcoming face. The man's intense eyes contrasted his cobalt skin as he glared at Jorge with hostility and pushed him into the wall.

"What are you doing in my shop?" the man asked in a fiery tone.

"I-I am Jorge. Jorge Milhouse Rodriguez Jr," he said, fearing what might happen to him. "I was going to look for money to give my brother so we can keep our apartment."

"You want shekels? Earn them like everyone else does, kid! Nobody robs David Corcrusteau!"

Jorge thought of how to handle the situation without irking this bellicose shopkeeper.

"The door downstairs…"

"The door, the door!" Mr. Corcrusteau mocked. "I used it to move some of my antiques into the shop. It leads to a rough part of town, so I wouldn't want to spend any more time there than I had to. What brought you there?"

"I told you, money for my brother."

"And I told you that if you want money, you need to earn it."

"Can I earn any here?"

Mr. Corcrusteau stopped to examine Jorge. After looking at his unkempt hair, his torn shirt, his bruises, and his face, Corcrusteau gave a vociferous laugh.

"I'll tell you what, if you with your ill little body can attract business and sell even a dozen items, I'll give you whatever you want!"

Corcrusteau was like all the others from back home who treated him with contempt. Jorge saw how this man judged his features rather than his character and determined this would be the last time. Instead of ceding to mock and pressure, Jorge accepted Corcrusteau's offer.

Jorge went to the outside of the building and gazed at its brown exterior. A dreary sign on top read *Corcrusteau's Antiques*. Jorge was told to attract business, so he decided the store needed to become more inviting. He traversed the disorderly basement of the shop, searching for materials to give this relic of a building new life. At last, Jorge stumbled upon a forgotten container of vibrant paint that captured the eye and was sure to lure in customers.

After hauling the container up the stairs and into

the mild heat, Jorge began his toil. He added a fine layer of gold and turquoise to the sign and added brighter bulbs to the lights inside the windows. Citizens passing through the area stopped and stared at him, impressed by the alluring colors he was painting and the determination with which he was painting them. When he placed some trinkets in the window to advertise the store's wares, customers entered the refurbished establishment and were again intrigued by the beautiful interior and unique products. Jorge manned a dusty register and rang up twice as many sales his new boss had required. Exhausted after his long day, he approached Mr. Corcrusteau about his payment.

"As per our agreement, I'll give you whatever amount you want." Corcrusteau paused. "Within reason."

Jorge did not recognize the currency the buyers used to pay, so he had to come up with a unique form of compensation. He glanced around the room and found the object of his desire, a gold pocket watch resembling the one back home. Mr. Corcrusteau rushed him through the door, which the contentious store owner boarded up on his end.

Jorge made his way to the apartment. Once again, the pedestrians exhibited their usual behaviors toward him, but he was unbothered. Jorge would no longer have his actions dictated by those who knew nothing of his character. He arrived late in the afternoon, barely beating Enrique home. When his brother walked in, he shared exciting news.

"Jorge! I have work downtown now! I won't get paid until the end of the week, but if…"

"Don't worry, Enrique," said Jorge as he presented the watch. "You can sell this until then."

Enrique looked to make sure their father's watch was still on the counter.

"Jorge, how did you get this?"

Jorge smiled, his large teeth gleaming as he did so. "I had work, too."

5

SOME THINGS ARE MEANT TO BE

ANNA CLAIRE JACKSON

*I*t was deathly quiet in the hospital. Among the rooms lay a girl in a bed with her family beside her.

"What?" my mother exclaimed. "Cancer!" Her sense of desperation was one only a mother could muster. Subdued sobs from everyone else in the room joined my mother's wails.

My mind raced, but I'm not the girl in the hospital bed. My sister, the beautiful Addy, didn't deserve this; it should be me, not her! Reality set in as I forced myself to focus on the voice of the doctor: "We need to get her into surgery right away." He continued to speak, but I didn't listen. For once, I had nothing to say, as overwhelming guilt consumed me. My sister should get to live her life to the fullest.

I must have remained in this state for a long time because my dad nudged me in the elevator. How did I get here? "Gwen, I'm going to take you home," he said, his voice betraying his weariness. My head swung up and down in an almost mechanical motion as I trudged to the car. "I'm sorry you heard that." It seemed Dad had more to say, but he changed the subject. "I'll drive you home. Even though you're old enough, you're in no condition to drive. Perhaps you could work on that book you're writing."

We exchanged goodbyes, and I dashed into the house sobbing, my body betraying my mind. After about an hour, my stomach growled, so I made my way to the kitchen. On the way, I walked to the bathroom to check my appearance. My eyes, normally a deep amber, were bloodshot red; my long, brown hair, a mess.

"Ugh, it's not fair!" I shouted as anger took hold of my body, causing me to thrust my draft across the room. I have no idea why I took out my rage on my story, but I had already committed the act.

I glanced at my books on the floor, picking up my favorite, *Little Women*. I couldn't help but notice the irony as I flipped through. The book landed on the chapter where Jo and Beth were flying the kite. *When Jo came home that spring, she had been struck with the change in Beth*. Beth would die that day. There was a closeness in that moment I couldn't quite touch, a feeling that I had no words to describe, but for once in my life, I understood the pain Jo went through.

Suddenly, the pages flipped by themselves; the book was going berserk! "What's going on!" I shouted. The book was creating a sort of portal, a blue vortex that appeared out of thin air. I jumped for cover, but the book's cover had other plans, swallowing me into its pages.

I landed on something cold. Snow? In the middle of summer? A busy street surrounded me. I knew this because the concrete of a sidewalk greeted me when I fell. Curiosity got the better of me as I opened my eyes to observe my surroundings. Pedestrians stared at me like an animal at the zoo. Embellished in extravagant winter coats, the passersby gave me the impression that this was the 1800s, possibly in New York, given the style of the buildings. What was happening?

I slowly stood up, but I hit the snow again with a loud thud, "Ow!" I cried, rubbing the arm that broke my fall.

"Oh, I'm so sorry about that! Here, let me help you up." Her eyes did the talking as her eyes fixed on me. Her brows furrowed ever so slightly. "Excellent outfit!"

I wore skinny jeans and a tee-shirt I bought from a state book fair a few years ago. The lady in front of me had wild red hair and expressive gray eyes. Wait, is she?!

"I'm Jo March," she said, raising a hand to me.

I shook her hand to be polite. "Jo... Jo March?" But how? Should I tell her about my situation? Of course I should. Then I can figure out a way to return to my family, who needed me as Jo's family needed her.

"I'm Gwen Bailey. You will not believe me, but I'm not from here..."

She cut me off, pointing. "Obviously not. Look at those clothes. I've never seen a girl—well, except myself—wear pants."

"Listen to me! I'm not from this world. I'm from an alternate reality. In my world, there's a book about you. I have no idea why I ended up here, but I desperately need to return to my sister. It's important." If the circumstances were different, I'd probably flip after meeting Jo March in person.

"Wow, you remind me of one of my favorite book

characters. Since I'm a book in your world, you could be a story in mine," she said, as if this whole situation wasn't freaky enough.

"Aren't you the least bit weirded out by this?"

"No, I'm an author. I fantasize about stranger things than this. This is nothing. Okay, now how do we get you home?"

"Good question. I've seen movies with plots like this. Why not try what they tried? Maybe we have to play out your story?"

"Great idea—but what is a movie? Never mind... what do we do?" She pondered for a few moments before continuing. "We need to go to Concord. I'm supposed to go home to see my family."

I decided against telling her about her sister Beth's eventual passing. "Okay, I was on my way there, anyway." I stifled a giggle of disbelief at the thought of my favorite character taking me to her home.

As a woman walked past us, staring at me, Jo said, "First, we should get you some new clothes."

We arrived at Concord after a train ride. Who could have imagined meeting your favorite character would be this much fun? Jo introduced me to her family at the point in the book where the only ones at the house were Jo's mother, Marmee, and sweet Beth.

After getting to know the two of them, Jo spoke. "I brought a kite. I'm going to take you two to the beach." She gestured to her suitcase.

"That would be grand!" Beth responded. I remembered what was about to happen, so I stayed at the March house. After they left, I prepared my emotions for what was to come.

It wasn't until the next morning that Marmee and Jo returned. I braced myself for the inevitable. Jo walked through the door and sprinted upstairs, with Marmee trailing her.

I followed Jo and screamed when she tore the first of her memoirs and notes. "Stop! This is tough, but we will survive it."

"You have no idea how it feels until you have lost a loved one," she said, struggling to regain her composure with me standing in her room.

"No," I said as tears formed. "I do. The doctors diagnosed my sister with a horrible disease right before I came here; she might not live long."

She released a soft gasp. "Then shouldn't you be home? Isn't my story over?" All at once, I understood what I needed to do. After the comfort Jo had provided me through the years, it was time to return the favor.

"Your story... it's barely begun. It's hard losing someone, but we can choose to drown in our sorrows, or we can choose to rise above and keep pushing through, even when we feel torn apart and hopeless."

"It was several days before Christmas..." she whispered, just like in the book.

I let out a sigh of relief. I had set the story back on track and comforted the character I most respected. We remained there together until she wrote all but the last sentence.

"What if no one reads it?" she asked, a glimmer of uncertainty resonating in her voice.

"Trust me, they will," I said, squeezing her shoulder.

"Alright, here goes." Jo finished the last sentence, and the familiar portal opened through the page.

"That's how I get home!" I shouted.

"But I need you when I try to pitch this."

"You don't need me. You can do this." I barely finished my sentence before the blue light engulfed me.

I faintly heard Jo say, "Thank you and just wait—

everything will turn out fine" before being completely consumed by the blue.

I disappeared from the attic and landed hard on the floor.

"Ow." I must stop falling onto the ground like this. Three hours had passed. My phone was ringing with a call from my dad.

"You didn't answer your phone. Are you okay?" he asked.

"I'm fine! You know me; I fell asleep," I reassured him.

"Okay. Well, good news. Addy did great during the surgery. The doctor said he's never seen a braver little girl. Don't you see? That's because of you, Gwen. You and your story inspired her!"

I breathed a deep sigh of relief when the call ended. Out of habit, I glanced down at *Little Women*. Thank you, Jo. No matter what happens, I'll stay strong. I picked up my memoir from the ground. Alright, here goes. I picked up my pencil and finished my story.

6

THE PERFECT WORLD

ALYSSA KINKADE

"Today has been the worst day of my life. Everyone keeps saying 'sorry for your loss' or 'she's watching over you,' but she isn't here with me anymore. It's crazy to think she won't be here to watch me graduate, get married, or hit any milestone a mother is supposed to hit with her daughter. I stand up here to say that my mother was a kind, loving, and selfless person who left us too soon."

"That was a lovely speech, Pumpkin. Mom would be proud," my dad says, pulling me into a hug.

"Thanks, Dad."

"I think we should go get some pizza and head home for the night."

"Alright, that sounds nice."

Once we're home, my dad and I watch my mom's favorite movies in my bed and stuff our faces full of barbeque pizza. At some point, I must have fallen asleep because I awoke to light shining through my window. As I go downstairs, I hear my dad on the phone in his office.

"I haven't told her yet, but it's for the best. She might like the change in scenery."

A change in scenery? Are we going on a trip? Just as I am about to walk away, my dad comes walking out of the office.

"Oh, hey, Pumpkin, how'd you sleep?"

"Yeah, Dad, I slept fine, but are we going somewhere? I heard you talking on the phone."

"Yeah, let's talk about it over breakfast."

For breakfast, we both have eggs and bacon. Once we sit down at the table, I notice Dad looks nervous. "Alright, so I'm just gonna rip off the band-aid and tell you. We are moving to South Carolina."

I can't believe it. We are moving from San Francisco, where I've lived my whole life, to South Carolina. "How soon?"

"Next week. And I understand you must think it's random, but when your mom died, we were given her family's house. But, hey, why don't you go hang out with your friends? I'm sure they have missed hanging out with you."

"Okay," I say as I leave the kitchen and head up to my room.

The next week flew by with hanging out with my friends Sierra and Luca,and packing up the house.

Today, though, is the day we move and leave my childhood home. I'm sad, but I think Dad is right by saying I'll like the change. After we finish packing the last of our stuff into the U-Haul, Sierra and Luca say their goodbyes to us.

We get in the truck and start our journey. We spend the next four days driving to South Carolina. Getting out of the truck was such a relief.

The house is a beautiful Victorian-style with three floors and five bedrooms. Once we get inside, Dad heads to the master bedroom to unpack, while I scope out the perfect room. I choose the light blue room with a balcony and a canopy bed.

Before I unpack, I give myself a tour of the place. When I get to the third floor, I notice an open door at the end of the hall. I step inside the almost empty room to see a beautiful gold-framed mirror. I run my fingers along it and my hand disappears.

As I push it further, more of my hand and now my arm disappears. I step through, closing my eyes, and I open my eyes to see women in ball gowns and men in tuxedos.

I look around at all the people in the ballroom dancing and laughing. A woman who looks familiar catches my eye. I follow her to see if I can get a closer look at this familiar figure. As I get close enough to tap her on the shoulder, she turns around and meets my eyes. I instantly recognize her face; it's my mom. She smiles and pulls me into a hug. "Oh, Finley, I knew you would find me here," she says while still hugging me.

"Mom, what is this place? Why are you here?"

"Well, darling, this is the perfect place, and I'm here because I want to be."

"But why leave me and Dad?"

"Oh, darling, it isn't like that. An opportunity arose, and I realized it was time to come back." She states this as if it makes her leaving any better. But before I can say any more, she walks off.

"Follow me." We walk down an elegant hall before stopping at a door.

Here is where she tells me all about this "perfect place." How everyone is happy and always having balls or events. She also informs me more about the reason she left, telling me she has been dreaming of this place since she was a kid coming here. When she found out where the mirror was, she thought it was perfect.

"Now, darling, you must change into your ball gown." She says this while handing me a blue gown.

Once I change, I meet Mom back in the ballroom and danced. I spent the next week there, dancing with all the people. Mom asked me to stay there with her dancing forever. But I remembered I had to get home, and I couldn't be away from Dad any longer.

While dancing with Mom, I blurt out, "You need to come back home." She laughed and said, "Honey, I belong here, not back in that boring world, and you belong here, too." She tried pulling me but it was no use.

"No, Mom, I can't stay here. I have a life to live, and Dad needs me."

"Finley, this isn't up for debate. You're staying here."

I had never seen this side of her, and I needed to get out of here. I pull from her again and manage to free myself from her grip. I run as she chases me. "Just find the mirror," I repeat to myself.

At the mirror, I look back at my mom. I tell her I would miss her and step through the mirror.

———————

I open my eyes to recognize I am back at the house. I run downstairs, find Dad, and give him the biggest hug ever. I tell him everything, and he seems calm.

"I always figured she'd go back and try to take you with her. Your mother has been obsessed with that place ever since we met. I could never go there since I wasn't blood-related, but I knew once we had a child, she would try to take you with her. That place is not somewhere safe; I'm so glad you're okay."

It surprised me that he had so much knowledge of the world and although I wish Mom didn't care more about a crazy world than me, I'm so thankful I have Dad to rely on. He'll always be my number one friend.

7

THE ELECTRIC GUITAR ODYSSEY
NOAH LEE

*T*imothy sat at his desk, trying with little success to write a rock 'n' roll song. He let out a heavy sigh. Unless he could create and sell a great song in the next week, he'd have to pawn his prized electric guitar. It was a red and white masterpiece that he had used in hundreds of jam sessions. He sank back into his chair and tried to keep writing. It was hard for him when his only inspiration was the ragged wallpaper and scratched wood flooring of his tiny bedroom. He had a window; however, the view was a dirty brick wall.

Timothy lay awake that night, thinking of his past failures, including that awful last gig he had performed. When he dozed off at last, a loud noise coming from his living room jolted him awake! He pressed his ear against his door. The commotion almost sounded like—music? He opened the door and a bright light emanating from the center of his living room blinded him. It was a brilliant, red-and-yellow flashing light coming from some object on the other side of the room. When his eyes adjusted, he realized the mysterious light was coming from his prized electric guitar. With tentative steps, he made his way over to the guitar, the music getting louder with every step. Maybe he could find out what was happening if he touched it. Timothy reached out and grasped the head of the instrument. As soon as he did, the wind picked up and blew gusts of air through his living room. The music, almost deafening, sped until the melody was no longer discernible. The bright light enveloped Timothy. Then, everything went black.

"Are you okay?"

Timothy groaned as he sat up. He jumped when he spotted the source of the voice. The creature talking to him defied the laws of science. It was a large brown dog that resembled a mascot costume. It had long brown ears and two big, genial eyes.

"Where am I?"

"Welcome to Musicland!" the dog replied.

"Musicland? For real, where am I?"

The dog walked over to his desk and picked up an official-looking document. "Allow me to tell you why you're here," the dog read. "Every year, we choose a promising young musician seeking inspiration from the earth to be brought to Musicland. When young musicians get here, we assign tasks to help find their inspiration. My name is Milo, and I am your guide. Your mission, whether you choose to accept it, is to journey into the Cavern of Artistry and retrieve the lost Totem of Inspiration. Do you have questions so far?"

"What?" Timothy exclaimed. "Of course I have questions. I'm talking to a dog right now! Take me home right now, you animal."

"First, call me Milo. Second," he continued to read, "the prospect may choose to leave Musicland. However, if you choose to reject your assignment, you will pass up the opportunity to become a renowned musician, like some of our previous prospects, such as Beethoven, Elvis Presley, and Michael Jackson. If you choose to complete your assignment, you will receive great wealth, talent, and fame."

Timothy's eyes lit up at the mention of the rewards. "You have my attention. When can I start?"

"Come with me," said Milo.

Milo handed Timothy a bag and together they walked. After a few hours, they reached their destination, a gaping hole in the earth leading down into a shadowy black abyss. Timothy had never liked heights, and the sight of the hole made him want to turn back. Still, he knew he had to keep his courage if he wanted the fame that the document promised.

"I think it's important that I make something clear to you now. As a guide, I'm not allowed to go inside with you. From this point on, you must continue alone." Milo paused. "With that being said, jump."

"What?" Timothy jumped back. "Are you crazy?"

"Jump in," Milo reiterated.

"I will not jump. That's suicide! There has to be another way."

"There is no other way. If you want to succeed at the mission, you must jump in, Timothy." Timothy looked down at the hole. Perhaps he was crazy, but his gut was telling him to jump.

"Okay, Milo," he said with surprising calmness, "Thanks for everything." Timothy closed his eyes, took a deep breath, and jumped. As he was falling, an otherworldly, high-pitched, beautiful sound filled the surrounding space. As he reached the bottom, the sound faded away, and he slowed to a near-halt. He had almost stopped before his feet hit the cold, uneven ground underneath him. He had entered the Cavern of Artistry.

When he landed, a thundering sound greeted him from an intricate arch. When he entered through the arch, he saw the source of the noise. In front of him was a large underground lake where waves would roll and crash into the cave's jagged walls. It was impossible to cross. As he was looking around, he stubbed his toe on something on the floor. He glanced down at what had tripped him. What was this? It seemed to be an electric guitar, the model he had at home, but made of crystal and gold. He picked it up and played a few notes. Those few notes led to a song, and before he knew it, Timothy was jamming out with this familiar guitar he had found. At the end of the final chord, a loud whooshing noise filled the room. The waters split down the middle and an enormous staircase appeared. When he walked down the stairs, he found himself in front of a door under a large engraving.

Here Lies the Totem of Inspiration

This was it! Timothy reached his destination, opened the door, and ran through. He landed in a different world, complete with ragged wallpaper, scratched wood floors, and a small window overlooking a brick wall.

He was... in his apartment? His closet door slammed shut behind him. He fumbled for the door's handle, trying to return to the magical world that he had just left, but when he opened the door, all he saw were shirts. He sat down at his desk. How would he ever get inspired now? He thought about his adventure. Would his effort produce a reward? As he thought about his adventure in retrospect, however, he remembered the music that he heard along the way. He recalled the ethereal melody he heard while falling, the thunderous cadence of the lake, and the guitar solo he had performed to cause the lake to open. He reached for a piece of paper to write it down. He had a new song!

8

SAVING JOSEF

SARAH MURLEY

I went to sleep starving. My mother disliked that word. She said, "Our family has a lot to be thankful for, even when life seems unfortunate. There are always enjoyable moments when you look hard enough." She encouraged my brother and me to stay positive during the bleak times.

"Eda!" My younger brother, Josef, shook me until I was awake. The small beams of sunlight peering through the window made me realize I had overslept.

"What's wrong?" His distraught expression concerned me. I thought of the terrible things that could have happened.

"Is it Mother?" Josef nodded, and we raced to her

bedroom. My mother lay on a small, dilapidated cot. I pressed my hand against her forehead. "Mother, your forehead is hot. Your fever has risen." Her skin was pale and her forehead had beads of sweat running down it, but she smiled. She always tried to remain strong for Josef and me, even though she wasn't in the best condition.

"A cold won't defeat me," my mother said. I heard my stomach growl. For a second, I forgot about our poverty. No matter how hard I tried to imagine my food as a good meal, I could never trick my body into thinking it was enough. "I don't think we have much food left. You can go to a food queue, but the lines will be very long. I'm sorry, you both deserve better than to go hungry all day."

After my father died in the war against the Allied Powers and my mother fell ill, I preserved the Krämer family. Being born into war and poverty ensured that I grew up fast. At fourteen, I took care of my sick mother, looked after my brother, and supplied food to the table. Many nights, we ate little. The government rationed food because of reparations from the war. If I didn't get to the queues, we didn't eat much. Although our situation was desperate, I refused to give in.

"Don't worry, Mother. I'll find us something.

You'll need sufficient food to recover and I bet some delicious potato pie would give you the energy you need. You'll also need food to grow, Josef. I didn't forget about my favorite little brother," I said.

He laughed. "Eda, I'm your only little brother." I loved seeing a smile on his face. I struggled to see the positive side of our situation, but I tried to pretend for Josef.

"Go clean yourself up while I talk to Mother. Do your chores, and I may feed you tonight." Josef rolled his eyes and left, and my focus shifted to our mother. It seemed like every time I looked at her, her spirit waned.

"I'm going out, and I'll be back soon. Will you manage?"

"Eda, I'll be just fine, and Josef is here if I need anything." I placed a kiss on her forehead, grabbed some marks, and exited the house. As expected, queues were full of desperate people. There would only be scraps by the time I received anything; however, there was an old bakery nearby. I wasn't sure if it was open, but I would not take a chance of missing out on food if it was.

I rushed to the bakery. I suspected I didn't have enough marks, but I had to try. Seeing the open sign made my heart leap, so I ran through the bakery door and scanned the shelves. The array of pastries was shocking to me, and the prices were expensive. I didn't have enough money.

I guess we're not eating again. There was no other way to get a decent meal. "Well, what if I. . .," My heart quickened as I looked around for the owner. *I knew stealing was wrong, but what other options did I have?* My stomach growled, coveting actual food.

I tried to walk away, but my feet wouldn't move, and I didn't want to face my family without food, or with stolen food. *If I returned empty-handed, then what would happen to them?* My mother was hanging on by a thread. A thread I feared would soon break.

"Eda," a familiar voice called.

"Father, how are you here? You died in the war." He walked toward me, and we both cried. I hadn't seen him in years. Since I was six when my father left, I had barely any memories of him.

"I'm here for you. Don't worry, little one."

"How am I supposed to provide for our family without stealing? I'm a dreadful person for even considering that. I'm scared and not cut out for this role. We need you back." My father remained silent.

"Is something wrong?" I asked. He shook his head and continued to ponder.

"Why don't I share a story with you?" His question confused me, but I nodded my head.

"It had been a year since I left, and some men rumored we might get leave. The thought of seeing you guys motivated me to keep going, so I promised myself I would do anything to see you again. War changed people, and I feared it would change me. One night challenged my morality and promise. They ordered us to destroy a camp, and the goal was to ambush them.

"Unfortunately, I ended up in the middle of the skirmish. I became separated from my group in the middle of the chaos. I hid behind some rubble, but I realized someone else had the same idea, and I killed the man. Every night after that, I dreamed of the French soldier. The memory of killing him replayed in my mind thousands of times. I felt immense guilt for killing him, but I had another chance to see my family. Even though I died soon after, I believe it was worth it for my country and my family. I would've done anything to protect my family."

I tried to speak, but no words came out. My father's experience of war was truly heartbreaking. He sacrificed a lot, and I wasn't able to provide for us. "I don't understand. How does this relate to me?"

"Eda Krämer, you've looked after our family all these years and stayed true to your virtues, so I'm advising you to take the food. It's not a black-and-white decision, but your mother and I won't think any less of you. You're doing it for your mother and Josef." He gave me a final hug with tears in his eyes. I hugged my father tightly, not wanting to let go, but slowly his arms slipped away from the embrace.

"Wait! I can't do this without you." A lump formed in my throat. Instead of turning back to face me, he merely walked away. I was alone in the shop with a tough decision to make. My father advised me to steal. Turmoil festered inside me, and my thoughts became entangled. My father killed a man, yet I still thought of him as a good man. *If I stole, would my family still look at me the same?*

After immense consideration, I swiftly exited the bakery door with a loaf of bread and a guilty conscience. No matter my feelings toward the matter, I knew it would help my mother and brother. I was doing it for them, just as my father based his actions on his love for us.

I made the right decision. They'll eat tonight. I arrived back at our dreary house, nervous about my mother's reaction to the food. The front door opened with a creak and filled the eerie silence. Josef ran towards me with panic in his eyes.

"Eda, help! Mother won't wake up!" The silence became more agonizing as I recalled the state of my mother when I left. I dropped the bread and ran to our mother's room. Her sickly appearance had grown even more severe. Holding her in my arms, tears fell like raindrops against my cheeks.

"Please, mother answer me."

"Will she be ok? I kept checking in on her to see if she needed anything, but she insisted I finish my chores. I came into the room to check in again, and she wasn't awake. She wasn't responding to me. Then you were nowhere to be found. I didn't know what to do. Eda, I'm sorry."

My grip on my mother grew stronger. "Please. I'm sorry I wasn't here. I brought food. We can finally get your strength back. I saw dad, too, and he would have wanted you to stay strong." I sobbed into my mother's chest, but her heart was no longer beating, and her breathing had ceased.

I've learned a lot from the past few days. My father made tremendous sacrifices for us, but in the end, he died. My mother did her best to raise this family, but sickness took her from us. I tried desperately to provide for my mother, but I couldn't save her. I'm fully responsible for Josef now, as he and I only have each other. So, I'll use my father's advice and my mother's determined spirit to raise him. I'm willing to go to great lengths to ensure my brother's future, just as our parents did for us. I couldn't save them, but I vowed to protect Josef. At all costs.

9

MARY AND ME
MCCAIN ROBERTS

I haven't eaten in three days and it's miserable. My stomach is always hurting and I can't find the energy to move. The camp is crowded, with no privacy, peace, or quiet. I'm a sixteen-year-old girl in a concentration camp full of people. Life can't get any worse. Every time I wake up, I wonder if I will live another day. I have no proper bed—my bed is on the floor and my back is in constant pain anytime I move. The Nazis struck fear into everyone since day one, which causes everyone to be scared to move.

You can't find a thing to do to entertain yourself except sit around and watch the days pass by and try to escape the notice of the guards. Sometimes, I wish my life would end, and I wouldn't be stuck in this terrible place anymore. Everywhere I go, hundreds of people surround me. Everyone here cries every day, wishing they didn't have to live anymore. The camp's worst location is the latrine. I walk in the door one day and realize this isn't the latrine!

Where am I? I've seen nothing like this—this place looks sort of like my camp, but newer. Why are there so many people? These are the same utensils I use at the concentration camp. Even the beds are the same. Where am I? I try to discover where I am when I notice a group of people walking.

"Hello, my name is Mary. Welcome to the Holocaust Museum. I am your tour guide for today."

The Holocaust Museum, I repeat under my breath. What is that?

I walk with the group for a few minutes while I try to listen and observe everything she says and does. There is so much going on! I am at a loss for words. Everything in this place looks the same as my camp. Everyone is asking questions, and I listen to them intently. I become more comfortable with the people around me, still unaware of what year I've traveled to.

I build up enough confidence to ask the kid next to me the question. He seems around seven years old, so I hope he wouldn't make fun of me for the question.

"What year is it right now?"

"It is the year 1994. What a dumb question," says the boy.

"I traveled fifty-two years into the future?" I say under my breath.

Now that I know I traveled into the future, I know it means I am here for a purpose. Mary tells her story as I listen with intense curiousity.

"I'm a survivor of the Holocaust. I became a prisoner in a concentration camp in 1942."

Wait, Wait a minute! Back in my concentration camp, it is 1942.

Mary continued, "Nazis captured me at sixteen, and I've never been more scared in my life. Every day, I lived in complete fear and tried my hardest to survive. One of the biggest reasons I had that fight was for my mother. She tried her best, but the Nazis also took her away. My mom tried to hide me under the stairs to keep me safe, but the Nazis found me. When they yanked me out, she tried to fight off the soldiers to buy me time to escape, but they shot her in the arm, leaving her there to bleed to death. She put herself before me, so now I am living on behalf of her."

After the tour, I pull Mary aside. "May I please have a talk with you? I'm not sure how I got here, but I'm here for a reason. I am also from the Holocaust. We have the same story and I think you might be me!"

Mary just stands there, looking worried for me, thinking I was crazy. "How is that possible? I'm sixty-eight and you are only…"

"I'm sixteen and I know it might sound insane, but I promise—you are me. Somehow, I entered something like a secret door, and it led me here. Our stories match up perfectly. I'll tell you one word only I would know: Barkley."

Barkley was the name of the imaginary friend who keeps me company in the concentration camp. Mary turns pale and seems sick to her stomach.

"Oh, my goodness, it is you… I mean, me!"

"How did you survive the camp? It is almost impossible!"

"One night, I stole a shovel from a worksite. Over time, I dug a tunnel at that worksite, disguising my work before we left each day. It took me two months, but it worked! Follow my steps, and you will survive."

"Thank you so much, Mary," ˌ
hands. "I will try my best."

———————

Once we say our goodbyes, I walk back intˏ
bathroom, and, sure enough, I am back in the caˌ
First, I find the worksite that Mary was telling mˏ
about. Once I find it, I dig for hours whenever I can
sneak away—day or night—until I am past the fence.
Once I'm far away, I dig up, out of the tunnel, and all
I see is sweet freedom. I make a run for it, thinking
about my mom and the future me. Thinking of her
gives me all the power I need. I run until I arrive at
the nearest town, where I find a family that takes me
in. They give me food and a home, eventually
moving away so I wouldn't be recaptured. Since
then, I don't worry about the Nazis because I am
safe and adopted into my new family forever.

10

THE LOCKER TO ALTERWORLD

JACK STEVENSON

*C*onnor packs up his stuff for the day and closes his locker. He really wishes the chemistry lab hadn't taken so long. Connor just wants to go home, away from those rich kids. It's not like they're ever mean to him or anything, but they probably don't want a poor kid for a friend. He walks through the empty hallway toward the stairs leading down to the ground floor, intent on going straight home and getting away from the rich kids he knows don't like him around.

However, while he walks down the dimly lit hallway, Connor hears a strange humming sound. Suddenly, the hallway lights shut off, and the only light remaining is a soft blue light emanating from behind an old locker. Even though his instincts warn against it, Connor reaches for the locker's handle and opens it, his heart pounding in fear and anticipation the whole time. He finds a mirror inside the locker. As he looks at his reflection, he sees how tired and pathetic he looks.

"That's just great. I look in the glowing mirror and all I get is a reminder that I'm poor. Wait, why's the mirror glowing?"

Suddenly, Connor feels a mysterious force grab hold of him as it pulls him into the mirror. He screams and tries to hold onto the edge of the locker doorway, but the force pulling him in is too strong, and he gets sucked inside the mirror. The glowing stops and the locker door slams shut.

Meanwhile, Connor screams as he falls down into a pit of bright lights before landing in a strange forest. After a minute of laying on the ground, Connor stands up and looks around; above him, he sees dragons flying through the sky and giant stone buildings embedded into the cliffs. In the distance, he sees a rocky plain full of giant crystals jutting out of the ground, with giant millipedes crawling around.

"Holy moly," says Connor.

"I know," says a disembodied voice. Connor looks around, hoping to see who brought him here. He sees no one.

"Who are you? Where am I?"

"I am sorry, Connor, but I can't tell you my name right now. To answer your second question, though, I would like to welcome you… to Alterworld."

"Alterworld? What's that supposed to mean?"

"Actually, It doesn't mean anything. I just liked how the name sounded when I built this place."

"You built this place?"

"To put it simply, Alterworld is my brainchild; I put this place together with nothing but my imagination. I wish I could tell you more about the locale, but we're short on time. Come to the High-Tower and we'll talk more. It's a big metal building. You'll know it when you see it," the voice says as it fades away.

Connor sighs and begins walking down the path through the forest. "It looks like I'm doing a quest now. That's just great," he says, annoyed.

Thirty minutes later, Connor walks through a seemingly endless desert, sweating profusely from the intense heat of the sun. He sees an oasis in the distance and sighs in relief, but he notices a lump of cloth laying in the sand in front of him. He walks over to the lump and turns it over, revealing it to be an old man passed out from the heat. Connor shakes him, stirring him awake. The old man raspily groans.

"Water, water," says the old man. Looking up at the oasis, Connor helps the man stand up, wraps the man's arm around his shoulders, and helps him walk towards the oasis. Once they reach it, they both sit down next to a pool and drink from it. After Connor finishes drinking, he looks up and sees the man looking at him.

"You saved my life young man. Thank you," the old man says, pulling out a golden necklace from a bag on his hip, "Take this. You need it more than I do."

Connor feels unsure about taking the necklace, not understanding why the man would act so kind toward him. He decides refusing would be rude and takes the necklace, putting it in his pocket. He walks out of the oasis, leaving the man to continue drinking.

Two hours later, Connor arrives in a grassland where sinkholes regularly open up to entire caverns. As he walks through the field, he spots a massive metal tower in the distance.

"Finally!" he cries out in excitement, not paying

attention to where he is walking. Connor accidentally falls into a sinkhole and lands in a cavern. He gets up and looks around, but a strange moaning startles him. He looks into a dark corner of the cavern and sees a figure slumped over. "Uh, hello?" Connor calls out. To his horror, the figure stands up and sprouts spider-like legs from its back. The figure emerges from the shadows, revealing a man with black eyes and fangs. Connor screams and tries to climb up the cavern wall.

"Oh my goodness, I'm so sorry! Calm down, kid! I'm not trying to eat you!" Connor stops screaming. When he turns around, he sees the man-spider rubbing the back of his neck. "Sorry about that. I don't get a lot of visitors down here," says the man-spider.

"Is that why you were moaning?"

"I have a hard time fitting in with the other man-spiders. I like puns and they don't, that kind of stuff."

"Sorry about that. Could you get me out of this cave? I have to finish a quest."

"Yeah, sure!" The man-spider shoots a line of webbing out of his wrist at the rim of the sinkhole. He hands the other end of the line to Connor, who uses it to climb out.

"Hey, before you go, could you spare me a pun?" asks the man-spider.

"Uh... sorry for *dropping in?*"

"Thanks, man!" the man-spider says, laughing. Connor continues his journey.

One hour later, Connor walks through the mountains, close to the High-Tower. As he walks along a stone path, he spots a Japanese-style archway, where a lone woman stands, clothed in a hooded robe with fire patterns. He spots heavy rain beyond the arch. As he approaches, he hears the woman crying.

"Why are you crying?" Connor asks. She sobs in response. Connor awkwardly hugs the woman, who slowly stops crying.

"Thank you," the woman whispers.

Connor lets go and backs up as the woman transforms into a red dragon. It flies up and breathes fire into the rain clouds, turning the rain into steam. Connor looks on, amazed, before continuing to the High-Tower.

Ten minutes later, Conor reaches the base of the gargantuan structure but finds no entrance. Suddenly, a beam of light appears around him, and he disappears. He now finds himself inside a well-lit, futuristic hallway leading to a cool-looking chair. It turns around to reveal… a regular guy. The guy stands up from the chair.

"Sorry about giving you the runaround, Connor. I'm the architect. You know, the voice guy. Great job on the quest."

"Okay, what the heck?!" yells Connor after a moment of staring at the architect in disbelief.

"Sorry, sorry, I didn't mean to cause you so much trouble. I was just helping you—,"

"What is all this? Why am I here? Why did you force me to walk for over three hours straight?"

The architect sighs, "Look, I know you don't feel you deserve friends, and I get it. I brought you here, put you through all those scenarios, to teach you. You're a good person, Connor, and you shouldn't think that just because you're poorer than the other kids, they won't accept you. You help people when they're down, even when they're different, and anyone would be lucky to have a friend like that. Now, I'll send you back home, but remember what happened here, Connor, and don't forget what this place has given you."

Connor hears a warbling sound and turns around to find a portal. He turns around to face the architect, who looks at him with a warm smile.

"Have a good day, buddy," the architect says as he gestures toward the portal.

Connor, with a tear running down his cheek, turns to leave. He walks through and finds himself outside the locker. He turns back to the mirror and sees himself smiling in the reflection. Connor closes the locker and walks to the exit, holding the golden necklace in his hand.

11

UNBEARABLY AFRAID

BAILEY STROUD

*a*s the bell rang for fall break to begin, my classmates bombarded me with questions. Ideas for a trip with my friends shot at me left and right. Someone suggested the idea of going camping. We took a vote, and I didn't voice my objections, but I was against the idea from the beginning. Not wanting to be difficult, I voted yes.

"Camping it is," I heard my friend say. I immediately regretted voting yes. The reason I didn't want to go camping had everything to do with an unhealthy fear of bears.

After packing several cans of bear repellent, I strapped into my mother's car. When we arrived at the campsite, all my friends welcomed me. As my mom drove away and the sun dipped over the horizon, the fear inside me rose. All night I was restless. I couldn't get images of vicious bears out of my head. The next morning, I was tired from not sleeping a wink, but the rest of the group was well-rested and ready for a full day of activities. I agreed to their itinerary because it meant so much to them.

We started our day in canoes. I was having a fun time canoeing because I wasn't thinking about bears. But after a while of rowing, my body screamed with exhaustion. I told everyone I was going to row back to shore because I needed a break. Just before I made it back, my sleep deprivation overwhelmed me, causing my canoe to tip over. Thrust deep into the water, I awoke with an icy sting from the river, and it woke up my body.

———

After fighting to the surface, I looked all around me, but I did not recognize my surroundings. I decided I'd get out of the water and check out my situation. As I started toward the shore, I looked down and discovered that my hands resembled those of a cartoon character. I glanced up, then back down again, only to realize that my entire body resembled a cartoon character. It wasn't just a regular cartoon...

I was a bear. I screamed at the top of my lungs. The next thing I knew, a large cartoon bear came walking in my direction. My first instinct was to hide, but while attempting to find a good spot, I heard someone calling me by name.

"Julie! Julie! I made lunch!" How did this bear know my name? I poked my head out of an animated bush, and to my surprise, I recognized a very familiar-looking figure. He saw me and scurried over to spread out a checkered picnic blanket. I tiptoed over and took a seat. He pulled out tea, honey, crackers, cheese, and salmon. I reached across the blanket and ate a few bites of his cheese. I still felt uneasy with my surroundings, but being starving and having nowhere to go, I stuck around for a few more delicious bites of food.

While we were eating, I questioned why this bear seemed so familiar. I eventually recognized him as one of the cartoon bears on Saturday morning television that I used to watch, but I was reluctant to call him by name. He told me he had something to show me, so after some initial hesitance, I followed him on a walk through the woods.

We came to a beautiful lake where he sat down on a nearby rock and asked me, "Look, do you see those bears over there?" They were eating honey out of a honeycomb. The bear explained to me that his kind likes honey and wild fish, and they dislike eating humans, a fact that calmed my nerves. He suggested I try to live life like a bear for a day and then decide if my fears were justified. To my surprise, he announced he had planned for me to shoot a movie scene with him. "Now this requires being around a lot of bears, but I know you can do it," he assured me. Even though I feared possible consequences, I couldn't avoid this. The cartoon bear had shown no aggression so far, which gave me some measure of comfort. In fact, he was rather nice.

As we continued to walk and talk, I lost track of time. At last, we turned a corner into what appeared to be a Hollywood set of all the old bear cartoons I had watched as a younger kid. All the bears smiled and waved at me, which I found cool, but still a little weird and unnerving. I kept reminding myself of what the friendly bear had told me and that they could only view me as another bear, not as lunch. As the day went on, I became more comfortable in my cartoon bear skin and got the hang of how bears live. The bears I encountered treated me with hospitality.

Maybe bears are nice, after all? Living like a bear is not so bad, is it? I had a great day. At sunset, I snuggled up in a warm cave with my new bear friends and drifted into a deep sleep.

I awoke at sunrise to the smell of bacon. As I peaked open my eyes, I realized I was no longer in a cave, but nestled up in my sleeping bag back at the campsite. I jumped out of the tent and exclaimed to my friends what I had experienced yesterday. They all laughed at me and swore they had been with me all day. They insisted it must have been a crazy, lucid dream. The rest of the weekend turned out to be the best fall break I'd ever had. I conquered my fear of bears and enjoyed a nice weekend getaway with friends. On our way home, I asked the group, "Who wants to go camping next year?"

12

THE FAMILY PORTRAIT
HALLE VINCENT

$\mathcal{L}$ovelyn working her after-school job at Sal's Burger Shop when she noticed Sal's office door open. She saw Sal's family portrait out of place; Lovelyn always loved that picture because it reminded her of old times. When she removed the picture from the wall, Lovelyn noticed a small hole that held a blue button. She pressed the button, but nothing happened. Lovelyn placed the picture back on the wall and returned to work.

That's when she saw him. She saw her dad.

On May 12, 2017, Lovelyn's father had passed away in a car accident. Her dad wasn't supposed to leave the house that day since he was off work. Lovelyn had left her homework at home, though, and called her dad to bring it to her. On his return trip home, a driver going the wrong way down a one-way lane near their house had collided with him.

Lovelyn ran to him, gave him a humongous hug, and told him how sorry she was.

"I'm sorry, have we met?" he replied.

"Yes, I'm your daughter!" said Lovelyn.

"I don't have a daughter."

Lovelyn sprinted out of the restaurant. That's when she saw a billboard that read *Join us this Saturday, October 28, for the annual Halloween Festival*. That's impossible. It's 2021, she thought. The last Halloween Festival had taken place before her dad had died. A million thoughts raced through her head. How did she end up here? How would she get back home? Was this a dream? Lovelyn's initial consideration was to return to Sal's since that's how she got to this place, so it must be the way back home. She ran back to Sal's office, but he wasn't there. Lovelyn expected she would just remove the picture from the wall, press the button, and things would return to normal. To her surprise, when she lifted the picture from the wall, there was no button behind it.

"What are you doing back here?" exclaimed Sal, appearing behind her. Lovelyn froze. She couldn't tell him what she was doing because if the button wasn't there, that meant this wasn't real, and Sal would assume she was crazy. She considered how her dad always found a solution, no matter how impossible a situation it might seem.

"Do you know where I can find Carter Thomason?"

"He just took off. He's not employed here, so I don't understand why would you look for him back here," Sal growled.

"Just wondered if he may have slipped back here. Do you know where he could be?"

"He may have gone home."

Lovelyn ran all the way to her grandmother's yellow house on White Lane and knocked. Her dad opened the door.

"What are you doing here?" he asked.

Lovelyn fell into her dad's arms and started sobbing. She told him everything—how it was all her fault he died, how that button was gone, leaving her stuck there. She produced a picture of him, her mom, and her.

Lovelyn's dad stood in silence for a few seconds

and said, "I believe you, so... how are we going to get you home?"

"I'm not sure."

"I think we should start by talking to Sal." Lovelyn noticed it was nine-thirty at night, so Sal would be gone by now.

"We can talk to him in the morning," said her dad. "You can sleep here until we figure out a way to get you back home."

The next morning, they went to Patty's Pancakes, which was their favorite restaurant when she was little. They talked about what life was like before he died and laughed about how he used to play "My Heart Will Go On" on the old jukebox at Sal's for her mom. This thought made Lovelyn tear up. Lovelyn's dad furrowed his brow and asked what was wrong.

Lovelyn paused. "Everything. Your being gone. Mom's being sad all the time. It's all my fault."

"Hey, I'm not aware of the details of what happened to me, but I'm guessing there was nothing you could have done to cause it or to prevent it."

"No, you don't understand! I'm the reason that person hit you. I'm the reason you're gone."

"There, you just said it. Someone else hit me, not you. Life is full of what-ifs. You can't live your life like that. Live with no regrets and realize bad things happen, and there is nothing you can do about some of them. I need you to promise to remember that."

Lovelyn smiled and promised she would. She peered at the clock, which read eleven o'clock—time to go to Sal's. They got up from their table and walked to Sal's. When they arrived, he was arranging tables in the front. Lovelyn's dad informed him he had something they needed to discuss with him.

"We can talk in my office," said Sal.

Once in Sal's office, Lovelyn's dad told him everything. Sal looked at him and started laughing.

"Is this a joke?" said Sal.

"This is no joke, Sal. Are you going to help us?"

"Well, I have no clue what you are talking about, so I suppose not."

"Don't play dumb with me, Sal!"

"I think it's time for you to go now."

"Don't do this Sal. Please, just help us."

Lovelyn moved toward the jukebox as they walked toward the front door. A token from it had caught her eye.

"Can I at least keep this?" asked Lovelyn, holding it aloft.

"Of course," replied Sal, still trying to shoo them out the door.

Lovelyn ran, instead, to the jukebox. She inserted the token and flashed a grin to her dad, who smiled right back. She pushed the button and spun back around to look at her dad, but he wasn't there. No one was.

Lovelyn ran to Sal's office to find him sitting at his desk. She asked him how long she had been gone, but he cocked his head to the side, clueless.

"No," Lovelyn said, panicked. "You don't understand. There was a button behind the picture, and my dad was here, and I talked to him. I was going to listen to our song."

"I have no idea what you're talking about," Sal replied with a wink.

13

SHE AND HER PEOPLE

EDEN WAGNON

*M*iddle school is a weird place. It is a place where we learn to lead or follow, and it takes courage, something I, Sia Davis, didn't have. The day I realized this began in the bathroom.

It was another boring day of math class, so I raised my hand in order to make my escape.

Mrs. Lynn must have thought I was asking an important question, for her face lit up. "Yes, Sia?"

"May I use the restroom?" I asked.

Mrs. Lynn's face fell as she let me go. As I walked down the hall to the bathroom, I stopped dead in my tracks when I heard banging noises coming from the bathroom. I barged into the bathroom and found a girl who is in my English class. Her name was Allison Jennings. Her head and hair were dripping wet. I noticed a gash on the side of her forehead. The girls standing over Allison turned around and smirked at me.

"You saw nothing!" the taller girl commanded me. I nodded, then scurried out of the bathroom.

My actions replayed in my head all day. Why didn't I say anything to help Allison? The shock and fear from earlier had turned into sickness and guilt churning in my stomach. How could someone like me find courage? That night, I opened my Bible. As I read the first sentence of the book of Esther, my vision blurred and spotted. The room spun and everything faded to black.

———

I opened my eyes to find myself in a foreign room that radiated riches. Chiffon fabric in bright shades draped from the ceiling and the bed I was lying in. I rubbed my eyes, only to find my hands a warm caramel color, and I knew something was off. I jumped out of bed and ran to the bathroom vanity, where I did not recognize the beautiful woman staring back at me. A servant girl entered the room and caught my attention.

"My queen, are you ready to get dressed for the day?"

"Queen? Are you talking to me?" I swiveled around to check the room.

"Of course. You are our beloved Esther, Queen of the Persian King Xerxes. It seems like a dream, doesn't it?" The woman grinned.

"Uh… yes… it does." The girl laughed at my response and then continued chattering to me about news and servant gossip as we got ready.

Afterward, I needed a place to think, so I inquired about the gardens to the servant girl. She gave me the directions, and I was off to my desired destination. I still had not understood how I had arrived in this world, and I wondered if I could ever leave.

After descending many sets of stairs, I made my way to the door of the outside gardens. The gardens were lovely with lush greenery and brilliant flowers everywhere. I crept deeper into the vegetation and sat on the bench in the back of the garden. I would sit and think here.

"Psst!"

I jumped up from the bench. "Who's there?"

A man crept from behind a bush. He whispered, "It's me, Mordecai. I come with news."

The name Mordecai sounded familiar. I muttered a greeting as I wracked my brain for where I had heard his name.

"Esther…"

"Esther?" Surely I wasn't the Esther from the Bible!

"Yes, this is urgent. Haman, the king's servant, has planned to have all the Jews killed on the thirteenth day of the twelfth month. We're running out of time. You must beg the king for mercy for you and your people." He really did not know who I was, for if he did, he wouldn't be asking me for help. If I couldn't even stand up for one person, how was I supposed to stand up for a large group of people?

"How am I supposed to do that?"

"Go to the king's court and request an audience with him. He might not receive you, and if that happens, they may put you to death. That won't happen to you since the king favors you so much." Mordecai grabbed my hands and gave them a squeeze. "The Lord will protect you if it is His plan to save us."

"What?! You mean I might die trying to save everyone?"

"Well… yes."

"Mordecai, I'm not as brave and bold as you think I am."

"Esther, you won't be able to do this alone. But God will grant you the courage if you ask him for it. Believe, Esther, and pray to the Lord. I must leave now, for I fear I'll get caught. Consider what I said, Esther. Be brave."

He went into the bushes and disappeared. How was I, Sia Davis, supposed to save the Jews? I knew what would happen if I didn't help them. I panicked.

"Lord, hear my prayer! I don't know what I'm doing here! How am I supposed to save the Jews? You must give me bravery if I am to save your people. Please protect me in the process and give me strength."

The next day, I asked my servant girl, whose name I learned was Daria, to make me look beautiful. If my looks made me attractive to the king, then it would not hurt to enhance them.

I soon stood outside the king's court, unaware of the source of the courage that welled up inside me. I waited as a guard entered the court to announce my presence.

"Queen Esther, sire."

I took a deep breath, then entered the court. The

king and I made eye contact, and the tension in the room increased. The king did not smile nor frown at me but remained expressionless. This was a bad idea.

"Lord help me..." I prayed silently.

The king broke into a grin and lowered his scepter. "What is it, Queen Esther? What is your request? Even up to half the kingdom, it will be given to you."

I returned the king's smile and bowed. "Your highness, I came to ask you if you would come to a banquet with Haman that I have prepared today." I tried to keep my voice from shaking.

"Yes, my dear queen." He commanded one of his servants to fetch Haman so he could fulfill my request.

Dinner wasn't as awkward as I expected it to be. The King and Haman didn't expect me to talk much and did all the talking themselves.

"Esther, tell me, what can I do for you? What you ask for will be given to you." The king smiled kindly. This was my chance to fulfill my mission, but it just seemed too early to tell him.

"If you join me again for a banquet tomorrow, I will tell you my request." If he refused, then I would confront him about the Jews now.

"We shall have another banquet tomorrow, then it seems!" The king exclaimed with a glow on his face.

The next day, Mordecai and I met in the garden. I told him of the king receiving me in his courts and how the Lord answered my plea for help. Knowing God was on my side made me happier and stronger.

"There's just one thing, Mordecai: I am so afraid to tell the king about the Jews and that his queen is a Jew. Will he be angry at me? Will Haman try to kill me? Tell me how to be brave!"

"Esther, the Lord has already granted you with bravery. Can't you see? He's allowed you the courage to approach the king, to ask him to dine with you, and to ask him to dine tonight. He is taking care of you, Esther." Mordecai smiled. "You're so close!"

"Oh, I never thought about that. In those times, I didn't feel brave. But the Lord carried me through, didn't he?" I grinned. "Do you mind if we pray together, Mordecai?"

"I would be honored."

We prayed, and then I returned to the palace to prepare for the banquet. Daria did my make-up, dressed me, and then did my hair.

"You know, you're much more kind than the previous Queen Vashti was. You're very favored in this kingdom, Esther." Daria said as she brushed my hair.

All too soon, I waited in the banquet hall alone for the king and Haman. I prayed a silent prayer to God for strength and bravery.

"Deep breaths, deep breaths," I repeated to myself. Soon the King arrived with Haman and we had a jolly feast. After Haman told a story of a self-righteous commoner, the king turned to me.

"My queen, what is your request? We made a deal, remember?" the king questioned. This was my chance to fulfill my mission. I took a deep breath.

"If you truly favor me, spare my life. And spare my people's lives. These are my requests. My people and I have been sold to be killed and destroyed."

The king's face turned crimson. "Who? Who would do such a thing? Tell me his name."

"It's Haman!" I exclaimed.

The king shook as he rose and stomped out of the room. Haman lunged at me, grabbed my shoulders, and shook me, begging for mercy. I tried to push him away, but then he grabbed my wrists, all the while yelling, "Spare me! Please!"

When the king came back and saw Haman grabbing me, his face turned an even deeper shade of crimson. He sentenced Haman to death. After Haman was taken away, the king's burning fury slowly faded.

When morning came, I entered the king's court. He received me, and I fell to his feet. I begged him to save the Jews.

"Your Highness, I ask you and beg you to save the Jews. I cannot stand by and watch them be destroyed."

The king nodded and turned to Mordecai, who came to replace Haman. "Mordecai, write a decree in my name on behalf of the Jews. Write what sounds best to you." He removed his signet ring and gave it to Mordecai.

So Mordecai wrote the decree and sent it out to the people of the land, and the kingdom and Jews rejoiced. The king, Mordecai, and the servants praised me for my boldness and bravery. I credited these attributes to God.

That night as I laid to sleep, I thought about how much I'd changed in the past few days. I've learned about selflessness, humility, and bravery. I soon drifted off into a deep slumber.

When I opened my eyes, I found myself back in my room. I observed my modern gray walls and curtains and my carpeted floors. The soft blowing of the air conditioning replaced the sweltering heat. My clock read the exact time I had opened my Bible. The whole time I was Queen Esther, time stood still here? I couldn't believe it. Everything I just experienced felt so real. Although I turned off my lamp to go to sleep, I didn't sleep a wink as my thoughts ran wild.

About a week later, I witnessed Allison getting picked on. The two tall girls were stepping on the back of her shoes and kicking her calves.

"Hey, stupid, nice sketchers! Did mommy pick those out for you?" one girl taunted.

"Leave Allison alone," I said. "Your cruelty toward her does not go unnoticed."

My comments did not faze the two girls. They smirked at me and burst out laughing when they looked at each other. They may not have taken me seriously, but at least they began walking away.

"Are you okay?" I asked Allison.

"Yeah, thanks for helping me out." She gave a weak smile.

No longer did I carry the weight of guilt. I felt

abiding joy in the Lord for granting me bravery and a new friend.

14

TO THE MOON AND TO SATURN

LAYLA WALL

*V*era flinched as the front door slammed shut. The girl looked up, hoping to catch her mother's eye, but all she saw was the back of her head as she rushed into her bedroom. Vera needed help with her algebra homework. In the past, her mother would have offered it before she even got the chance to ask.

Many things had changed around the house since the passing of Vera's brother four months ago. Since then, the longest conversation she and her mother had was about a trip to the grocery store.

At fifteen, Vera looked almost nothing like her eleven-year-old brother, Sirius. Their only common feature was their sandy brown hair, and yet her mother couldn't bear to look at her. It was taking quite a toll on Vera.

She walked upstairs after putting her unfinished homework in her bag and passed her brother's closed bedroom door without stopping. She'd barely lain down when she heard a car pulling out of the driveway. Her mother didn't go many places these days besides work, so Vera rarely got the house to herself. She was always too scared to walk to her brother's room while her mom was just downstairs. She was almost too scared to do it now.

Vera took the few steps to her brother's room. She wanted nothing more than to open it and have Sirius tell her that she needed to "learn how to knock." She twisted the knob and stepped through the door.

———

When she saw wildflowers where her brother's bed and closet once were, Vera thought she was dreaming. She especially thought she was dreaming when she turned and saw Sirius standing in front of her. Vera's breath caught in her throat as she ran to hug her brother.

"Good seeing you too," he gasped. That is when

Vera knew it was real. She pulled back from Sirius with wide eyes.

"How?"

"I don't know how. But I *do* know why." Sirius sat on the grass and Vera followed suit.

"You haven't spoken to Mom in three months, Ver."

"*She* hasn't spoken to *me!*" Vera had forgotten how easy it was to argue with an eleven-year-old.

"I'm aware." Her brother raised his arms in a surrendering motion. "But she's not here, is she? You've got to try."

Vera sighed. She'd spent the past few months so angry at her mother, and now he was asking her to forget about it? Sirius glanced at her with pleading eyes.

"Don't look at me like that. It's not fair." She could feel herself caving in already. "What if Mom doesn't want to talk to me?" She had already lost her brother, and she intended to hold on to her mom for as long as possible.

"You know she does, Ver. She's just scared. She already lost one child."

"Who died and made you king of wisdom?" Vera laughed. Sirius gave her a funny look.

He stood up and smiled. As soon as Vera stood, he wrapped his arms around her.

"Talk to her, please," he whispered before pulling back. Vera nodded.

"I don't want to go back without you."

"I understand. But you have to." He hugged her one more time while fixing his gaze over her shoulder. His bedroom door was sitting behind her in the clearing.

Vera put her hand on the knob. She stared at Sirius and as she pulled it open, he said, "I love you."

Vera closed her eyes after one last look at her brother.

———

When she opened her eyes, she was back in the hallway. She let herself cry for another moment before going in search of her mother.

She found her mother in the kitchen unpacking groceries. "Need some help?"

Her mother's head shot up at the sound of her voice. She stared for a long while before Vera sighed and reached for a bag.

"We have to talk, Mom. This isn't what Sirius would have wanted." Vera glanced up and saw her mom's eyes filling with tears. Just as she was getting ready to leave and shout *"I tried!"* at the sky, her mother grabbed her hand.

"I know." That one little sentence meant the world to Vera. She squeezed her mother's hand in her own. "How about you go change, and we can go out for ice cream like we used to… and really talk?" Her mother sounded unsure, but it was a start. This was the longest conversation they'd had in four months, and that alone was exciting to Vera.

Vera rushed upstairs to change her clothes and put on a charm bracelet her brother had gotten her. She ran out of her room, but before she could step on the first stair, she turned around and walked back. Stopping in front of her brother's door, she knocked twice.

"Love you, too."

ABOUT THE AUTHORS

At the time of publication, each of the authors of this anthology were tenth grade students in Mr. Al Ainsworth's English class at Northpoint Christian School in Southaven, Mississippi. They completed this short story collection through a grant from the DeSoto Excellence in Education organization.

Eli Bailey

Hailey Brown

Jr. Bunch

Ethan Herrod

Anna Claire Jackson

Alyssa Kinkade

Noah Lee

Sarah Murley

McCain Roberts

Jack Stevenson

Bailey Stroud

Halle Vincent

Eden Wagnon

Layla Wall

Made in the USA
Monee, IL
02 March 2022

91957684R00066